"why the moon is quiet"
a collection of poems by Morgan Rosati

....

A thank you to my mother, for introducing me to writing and
instilling a love of words from my earliest memories, and anyone who
has given me an idea for a poem, whether consciously or not. I am
ever grateful for you and the memories we have made.

"lovebites"
Cold fingertips brush my neck; you caught
tendrils of my hair in rough calluses,
and goddamn did you pull.
But I swear, never have I felt anything so vividly.
Never have I wished for pain like I've desired
your worn hands, your nibbling teeth. My skin felt
undiscovered until you blazed a trail, the landmarks you leave
make me feel alive.

"hooked at first bite"
Someone asked me if
anything had happened between you and I
and I laughed, because they made the topic of us
seem romantic, when actually you are the forbidden fruit
which I, Eve, desire to eat,
and that should not be lauded, but scorned-
not a thrill, but a sick twist of guilt.
But, my stomach feels fine, and
my tongue still craves your skin.
If I could enter the garden again,
I would continue to choose to
disobey the natural law,
introduce my taste buds to sin.
They seemed confused by my response,
and I left them hanging-
no one needs to know I cannot possess self control
as I wait to give into temptation,
wait to be exiled from heaven.
I wasn't destined for good anyway.
It's interesting to ponder how much I used to care
compared to the amount I care now-
morals defeated, apathetic to the core
you are the apple of knowledge
and I was hooked at first bite.

"grow wild"
Let the roots of your imagination
grow wild and bloom colorful ideas.
Do not prune your sense of childlike
wonder, for it is
the joy of watching leaves unfurl over time,
for reveling in falling snowflakes,
for blushing when lips touch that keeps
the fire inside you alive.
Do not let the passion in your fingertips
and the
inspiration under your eyelids
wither and die.
Grow the gardens of your mind wild.

"my solar system"
The unearthly sensation of thinking about you
leads me to ruminate two possible futures.
In one, you and I collide like asteroids,
passionately exploding and reforming
as one conglomerate being. The other,
we are rogue planets,
once firmly in each others orbit,
now slowly drifting away.

Dear you,
I miss you
as my glass of water melts-
leaving tracks of
"When will you be back"s
and "Where are you going"s
on the dirty table.
My stomach pangs
because no, I didn't eat a good
lunch.
I was catching up on
schoolwork
dreams of your arms caused
me to miss. And supper?
Oh the irony!
I was patting on sexy eyes
and kiss me lips
for you, that, in the heat of the
room, melt and fade.
I miss you,
and you're in the next room.
I idly sketch on a napkin and
calculate how long a bracelet
would take to fall from your
wrist-
as long as it took me to slide
from your waist?
I'm no longer a trophy,
just a scuffed figurine waiting
on your return.
I miss you
even as you leave me to sit
and stare at the flood of
hurried "I love you"s

and "I'll be right back"s
leaking from my drink.
My awkward silences
and averted gaze
and sporadic hand gestures
lower your
carefully cultivated cool vibe.
My quiet demeanor reflects
the amount of information I
know about the things your
friends argue over-
and that is nothing.
I miss you
but you won't be back
until the magnet in your heart
pulls you to me.
And as gravity
slings you towards me
I hope the attraction never
fades,
Because you are my bus ticket
to the big city,
and even though I sit alone
tonight, I know if I call you'll
appear, and I'll slide you
through the social slots
looking as graceful
as a bouquet of flowers on a
counter- not a fragment of a
girl sipping her drink and
writing on splotchy napkins,
leaking apologies and "it's
okay"s
across a table.

"Complicated"
I am not complicated.
Pull one thread, and you will
unravel me like a sweater.
Nor am I a geometric proof,
containing a dozen ways to the solution.
There are no missing variables to my equation.
Why then do you pluck my threads in
multiple directions, questioning my sentences?
Why do you stare at me like I can't be solved, like
 I'm unexplainable? It is not I who is complicated,
 really, but you.

"loneliness"
Lonely is reaching across the sheets for
someone who's never slept there
and waking up to realize they still aren't there.
Lonely is tracing your lips in silence in the dark,
reliving the dream you know was real once, but
cut off before you got to the best part.
And I admit, as my eyes slid closed
around three am this morning, I was lonely.

"Did you make me care?"
I took sweaty glasses in my hands,
last night
smelling acrid death; liquid fire slid down my throat–
I spun a cocoon of incoherence like it was nothing.
I woke up on a gritty, sticky floor
this morning
stained blouse; nauseous, with a funny taste on my breath–
I walked out of the door like it was nothing.
I watch the disappointment cloud your eyes
right now
stumbling to you for a hug; my heart quivers
and slowly sinks into the roiling acid of my stomach.
Mistakes feel like something now,
and I'm not sure why.

"annoying habits"
It used to bother you, the way I would
bite my lips 'till they bleed, the way I pinch my nails
to my palms to hold back tears,
the way I tilt my head to respond,
effectively hiding the whirlwind inside.
At the end, you screamed that if I build walls around myself,
I will never have a relationship that works-
I tossed my hair and walked away,
unaware of the curse clinging to my back.
Now lonely nights break over my head like waves-
my walls became a cage slowly
filling with toxic waste and no amount of lip biting can
save me now.

"change of color"
Once upon a time
I stretched my fingers to the sky
and colored in lovely hues
of pinks and purples and blues.
My favorite colors
to start the day off right.
Just me and my sky
and the color palette marked
Crayola 126.
Now I sit in front of a computer screen.
The only colors I work with
are broken fonts
of black and white
and infinite tints of gray.
The rhythm of words
penned to paper like captured butterflies
for the reader to admire.
Just me and my solitary thoughts
and the open document marked"Untitled"

"a lesson more valuable than daisy petals"
When my daughter discovers the magical
properties of plucking petals,
I am going to take her hand, look into her eyes,
And say-
If wishing on daisies fails you, do not worry.
If he loves you, he will be
handing you the flowers. If he doesn't,
 you won't have flowers in the first place.
Love can be a cruel thing, Babydoll.
It will look beautiful like the flowers you pick. But
eventually love might wilt, no matter how you cling
to your bouquet. No matter the case,
if your flower petals fail you, do not worry.
He didn't deserve you anyway.

"winter blues"
Smother me in springtime until I feel sunshine again.
I can't tell whether my fingers are blue because of the cold
 or poor circulation or
the thoughts crowding my fingers eager to escape:
as smudged words on paper,
as stark lines of type,
incarnating into anything else
but the mess of my imagination.
I can't swim or sink; I'm frozen
in the pit of my empty stomach,
and flowers are as foreign of an object
to me as warmth and laughter.
I have to wonder,
when winter ends and springtime comes, will I thaw?

"because I'm blind and you're rich"
Secrets once clustered like gems in my irises.
When my eyes first caught the light, I fleetingly wondered
if you saw them glimmering, if
the hidden knowledge sparkled.
I didn't have to ponder long; you gouged
my treasures out and mined them into cold, hard fact.
Now I'm blind, and you're rich. Sometimes
I press my empty eyelids, contemplating
If I will ever see you again.

"she changed with the weather"
You long to take her hands
out of her pockets one last time,
and hold them in your own, stroking her soft
fingertips that are always cold.
You want her frown to dissipate like the clouds
at the end of a rain storm, to smile like a rainbow
shining in the sky.
But alas, you let your vibrance fade once.
Her dark clouds still remain,
and she carries an umbrella everywhere. She doesn't look
at the sky anymore. She won't be fooled into
temporary sunshine again.

"red bench"
Today on a red bench
I sat next to a woman waiting for a bus.
She was talking on her phone,
Irritation creased into the folds of her skin.
She waved her hands like she was casting a spell
of understanding for whomever she addressed.
In some part of my mind,
I wanted to reach over
And smooth the annoyance from her clenched shoulders
I'd say "It's okay, they don't deserve your precious time."
But like throwing rocks into a pond,
instead of creating ripples,
the idea abruptly sank
and she trotted onto her bus.

"why i'm constantly itching"
How I long to peel off the layers-
to scratch aside the skin you touched,
to burn the hair you stroked.
You are gone, yet your fingers have touched my skin,
and the prints will never fade, even if I shower
in scalding hot water. They say I am to blame,
and yet they don't see how
I wear your haunting like a hood, hiding the emptiness
that accompanies dark lonely hours
with nothing but the creaking of your absence.
I beg to fling aside the layers, yet I cannot live without them-
the memories of you tainting my lips,
like the smell of stale vodka on my breath.

"she heard bad news today"
vacant eyes gazing at Deep blue skies,
purple hands curled around her ribs.
brain tumbling in her Empty skull
unable to process what she has heard.
the Nightmare evolving from her past dreams,
ears to brain to tears to shakes to Screams.
they sent her home where Numb shock set in.
now she sits in her chair Cocooned in a blanket
sheltered from the Bad news, from the world.
staring out the window,
Vacant eyes gazing at deep blue skies.

"write my name"
in grade school
I would forget to write my name on my homework
and my teacher would punish me
"Every assignment you didn't write your name on means fifty times."
fifty times writing my name on a
blank sheet of paper as blank as my mind.
Now sometimes
muscle memory kicks in, and I take the scraps of paper
no one needs or wants, scrawling my name on them
over and over and over and over and over.
It claims something that's not even mine
expresses my frustrations without saying anything at all.
Anger concealed
in the mountains of the M,
Mindlessness looping
within the oval of the O,
boredom ricocheting
into the indecisive R,
upset thrashing
into the curve of the G,
Contentment sifting
into the angular bubble of the A,
and
Daydreams squiggling
into the swoops of the N.
In grade school
I would forget to write my name on my homework
and now I forget how to write everything
but my name- feelings lost within six letters
that mean nothing at all

"riding the wheel of feeling"
I am at the bottom of the wheel.
lately I've been hovering near the middle
"fine"- if you will, existing,
allowing myself to inhale and exhale.
I squirreled away chunks of time
as if stockpiling minutes when I'm "fine" will
sustain me when I'm at the bottom
and allow me to breathe,
even when the wheel on top of me
caves in my torso.
I say words past the pressure on my throat
but I'm really on autopilot,
focused on the force of the wheel crushing me
as I apathetically wait for a rotation, the
release from the heavy empty feeling
as I creak towards the top again, back to the
"joyful" state I constantly project
but rarely experience–
For now however, I linger until
my overwhelmed bones crunch
as the cycle continues, dragging me with it.

"you will be there"
My hair will forever hold your scent.
I can't get away from it, just like
I can't get away from you. Whether you're
locked in my words or ripping my heart to shreds
in the corner, pressing dark circles
beneath my eyes and coaxing guilty twitches
in my fingers. Isn't it the fate of a ghost anyway, to haunt the one
who ate away at their sanity?

"wearing your (favorite) t-shirt"
It's like wearing your favorite t-shirt.
Comfy, not very fussy, yet the
feeling of pure bliss lasts
as long as the fabric kisses your contours,
hides your flaws beneath protective billows of fabric.
This is what being in love with a best friend feels like.
Filled with reassurance that if the shirt wears thin,
if the memories threading the seams of the shirt
hang threadbare, it will steadfastly wait for another wear.
You love to include both in bed-
worn cotton caressing your shoulders as
warm fingers stroke your thighs.
Both promise tranquility and good sleep.
When you realize your favorite t-shirt is dirty,
You are just as content with washing it as
you are talking out a problem to your lover
knowing both will last through the process.
Both remember how you grew with them,
fitting into significant moments of your life.
This is what being in love with a best friend feels like,

"(endless) merry-go-round"
From one to the next to the next.
I spin around on a merry-go-round that
takes me to him and him and another him.
(The more I get, the emptier I feel.)
His lips and my hips and the numbers rolling
effortlessly off my tongue, his, mine, they combine and then break.
(Here I go again.) No matter how many times
I fall asleep beside them, I know one day
I will wake up, my hands will search the covers,
(and I'll be alone.)
No matter how many times I can let my conscience fade,
I know one day I'll look down
and my faults will be written at my feet.
The problem is, I can't make myself care.
It feels good to want and be wanted
without the broken heart of
tomorrow looming over my head.

"Gypsy"
The wind catches my legs, and I ride the breeze.
I'm a dreamer, a gypsy of sorts gusting about with the millions
of unheard wishes. My umbrella caught the updrafts
and I drifted along, submitting
to the overbearing Wanderlust
that comes from
staying in deep space too long,
from breathing the stardust in the clouds.
Somehow, scuttling across the sprinkling street
with matted hair and messy mascara
in my slick yellow coat
and daisy rain boots,
you noticed me
and caught my attention.
Your friendly "Hello!" disrupted my orbit and
anchored me to earth like a fallen satellite.
As they say, one thing led to another.
I rested in your arms and thought I had full grasp of my desires.
I was happy until I realized you had trapped me,
winding the silky ribbons of my dreams
around your fingers
as mindlessly
as I would wind a constellation around mine.
You distorted the weave of my perception,
replacing love with lust
as your mouth touched mine.
You sucked me towards you like a black hole.
Summoning courage, I bit my way free.
Spitting blood, I began to drift away
as you stretched out your Hands
to find a broken umbrella resting
against the concrete,
daisy boots sprawled down the length of two blocks
and a slick yellow coat lying on a bench.

"friend"
How curious to feel skin so familiar–
I knew you since the days
of popsicles on the playground swings–
yet so foreign, because I'd never thought of you this way,
the pounding heart, gasping breath,
lips devouring my neck.
Marooned on the island,
you were water quenching my thirst, fire licking my cold skin
warm. I let the flames wash me clean,
the water soak into my lips.
As I lay among the sun rays, the afterglow,
I wonder at how easily we blurred the lines of friendship.

"rot and decay: exhibit a"
Ghosts of insults past
cluster under my fingertips, snagging on my nails
and turning them yellow. The essence of you
reeks on my skin,
potent and cloying. The old I love yous blotch my cheeks,
hectic red dots spreading like a disease.
As I look in the mirror
with promises knotted in my hair, yesterday's grimace,
and the fat sliced from my bones,
I realize how filthy we truly were.

"going my own way"
We have fallen apart. People once knit together by late nights
and endless conversation
unravelled into separate units, each confined to their own room.
I predicted this once, sitting by the fire with him.
I declared that everything would fall apart.
The instant his lips touched mine, I knew
the journey ahead meant nothing but blisters.
Those blisters have calloused now, as I hang on
by the split ends of my hair, of our companionship
 as we prepare to separate not only by rooms, but miles-
never to speak of each other again.

"(un)passionate backseat trysts"
When two bodies interlock, is it wrong if
no love entwines them? If romance rots into lust–
convenience parked in broad daylight
with no shame or commitment?
We may not be Romeo and Juliet, yet
our lips form a more pleasurable dialogue.
Love evaporates in body heat and what's left will
hold me over until we burn out and part ways.

"6:47 A.M."
I roll over in bed. You are not here
and my fingers feel like lead, yet
They reach across the sheets–
searching
hoping to find your warm body.
Instead, they find my phone.
I sigh, and check the time.
It's bright out but
sleep invades my body in a hostile takeover
coiling in the knots of my bedhead.
Thanks to falling back,
I no longer am sure of the hour.
Peering at my screen,
my pupils slightly dilate and
a small bubble of sunshine bursts
when I read your name–
A poor substitute for your smile.
But I'll hold your words
to my heart– a schoolgirl
holding a love note to her chest,
hopeful and elated
feelings radiating through my fingertips.
The blissful glow intensifies as I read the message
"I don't think I'm drunk,
but it's 5:07 and I'm not
with you and that feels
like a fucking crime"
I sigh, let my fingers rest where your
body would be and roll back over
letting the warm tendrils of sleep
entrap me once more.
I let the words
play a chorus as I smile once, then fall
asleep.

"a tiring routine"
Passion is pointless. An endless wandering
through the different warm bodies I inhabit.
I don't even care to
talk afterward, just mindless tracing
the skin on his arm, awakening
to leave with my clothes
On the floor/in my arms/backwards and inside out.
I scamper back to reality light as a mouse,
careful not to disturb the already-built relationships.
Even though William Steinbeck says
the best laid plans of mice and men sometimes go awry
and perhaps the bomb will explode (again?).
Until this I let myself go through the motions-
a purposeless path, one guaranteed to disappoint,
endlessly meandering through the different warm bodies
I encounter.

"once she was a supernova"
A bottomless pit gathers
in the empty caverns of my heart,
ready to suck away any sustenance
daring to enter the chambers.
See how holey my lungs have become?
I have wormholes for each one of them,
the ghosts behind my shoulders,
hands clutching my arms.
Don't move, they whisper as I lay in bed, drowning the sheets in tears,
unwilling to own my existence.
Don't move, and
the universe can't hurt you any more.
I have laid in bed for hours staring at the ceiling,
wondering why I continue
to lay there when all the heavy weight of those vanished crushes my
skull. My brain echoes with silence
sometimes when the thoughts dry up, a deserted ruin of
ideas that almost once were,
that I tossed out when all the motivation left.
I am a black hole, negative space sucking in everything around it,
forcing people to come close
to crush their life force.
Winds prowls the dips in between each of my ribs, curls around my
hip bones.
One day, the bottomless pit will overwhelm,
and I will implode, devastating the cosmos around me.

"A Breakup in Five Minutes or
Less"
Minute number one
I love you.
If I could stretch a minute
between my hands,
I'd pinch the seconds in which
you opened your mouth and
expressed affection
and yank them out of line like
plucking beads off of a
necklace, even
knowing the string will break
and the space-time continuum
will end.
I would race through
wormholes to find the exact
point in time your brain
decided to
let your lips open and declare
your feelings and place that
moment in a glass jar to
observe it.
Minute number two.
Fuck you
Smash all my belongings
All the hidden nanoseconds
will surely be forgotten then,
stuck to empty bottles
 I've collected like residue-
fogging the glass, reappearing
no matter how many times I
wipe the surface. There is not a
single cleaning agent to
eradicate the time you stained-
I'm stuck with our-your, my-
mess.

Minute number three.
I miss you
Multitudes of lonely seconds
between my hands feel limp,
unwanted.
Why do I single amounts of
time out?
Portioning has no purpose,
except to
Measure the time in which
things fall apart.
Increments of milliseconds
quickly add up to become one
big fiasco,
and here it happened- the
commemorative sign reads,
"Here we were happy."
and I run my hands over the
letters
And remember how that was,
what happiness was like.
Minute number four
I can't get over you.
Memories like knickknacks
clutter my drawers,
Little hours of happiness
hidden away
as we hid in the basement-
trying to pretend we were the
only people,
Attempting to forget the seven
billion others.
Time moved with our bodies,
 sliding into every nook and
cranny

Sometimes I can almost still
feel your hands tracing my
contours.
Minute number five.
I will live without you.
Time will pass, dragging me
with it, like an opened
parachute
Only I never wanted time to fly,
I tried to stop the clock for you.
But here I am, outside, the
world is bright,
and I am alone.
Free but for the rope tied
around my wrist, pulling me
into another day that you will
not occupy ,
One in which I will hold
moments in my pockets
And dispense them like mints
to passerby,
Hopefully dispensing your
memory too.

"why bad girls act tough"
A bad girl never "gets the guy".
She prowls along the sidelines, slinks around the gutter.
Unless someone desires an adrenaline rush,
the coveted hush of secrets between lips biting lips
and hips dominating hips, she is never
called out to play. Once the night is over,
she returns to the bench, unsatisfied.
Unfortunately, she must always
play it cool, maintain subzero apathy.
How can she contest her feelings
when she is perceived to have no heart at all?

"reasons the conversation dies"
I cannot help but withdraw into my head;
no matter if you sit five inches or five feet away,
if it is you and I or all of our friends,
I always end up inside my own thoughts. You might think,
No, I know you like I know myself.
I think I'd know you outside of these four walls.
You're open, obnoxious, and opinionated-
actually, I prefer slipping into my mind, with what feels like
a constant stream of voices. I listen to music
to drown them out, but you can only kill so many
before they adapt and breathe underwater.
A lot of the time, I miss key points of conversation
and forget to tune in to your voice
and yes, I never remember your secrets because I don't hear them.
It is near impossible for me to listen, enough that
after you say your required amount of words
and it is my turn to say mine, I never have things to say.
I can't contribute anymore to your sprawling theories
any more than the weeds in the cracks of the sidewalk
Outside of our house.
And so we sit in silence, letting the air molecules
bounce and the house creak around us.
This is why the conversation grows stale,
why the flow of words dries up.

\

"beyond body parts"
Beneath my smooth throat lies a voice.
Even though they kissed you feverishly last night,
my soft lips hide opinions, purpose beyond
brushing your neck.
My "pretty" eyes conceal last night's dreams.
You love to grab my hips, but I doubt you know
they are the object of daily contemplation in front of a mirror.
Ample breasts cover my frantic heartbeat and years of thud-thud
and they will provide not only pleasure but nourishment someday.
The hands that love gripping your shoulders
also enjoy grabbing pencils and writing down poems in the dark.
Beyond my body crouches a personality,
hidden within a cage of muscle and bone and skin.

"why the moon is quiet"
Last night, in the spaces between
velvet black and morning,
I dreamt that the moon resented the sun.
The moon's luminescence
relies solely on the sun's rays.
Thus, the moon is trapped;
she realizes freedom means darkness.
Suspended in the sky; she mourns
her fate- doomed to dependence,
to shining with another's light.

"the best gift you gave me"
It was fragile–
A flower
opening slowly,
a woodsy aroma captivating my nose.
Soft petals embrace the air
touching my lips with absolute certainty.
I leaned back, assessed the colors
whirling
behind my eyes
And realized
I am selfish, I want another.
leaning in again.
I pressed you
like a flower,
between the pages of my lips
You open your bud
and slide in a flickering brush
of pollen
and my cheeks stain red
Against the gift
of your kiss.

"read me"
My cheeks flush and my finger tips ache–
longing to scrape down your spine, to
grip your hair as you open me like a book
and delight in every word. You hate to read,
but you peruse my chapters without
missing a syllable.
Your name sighed from my lips
as I pray that you wear my pages thin;
I want you to read me until my binding breaks.

"ritual"
How quiet. The house sits
silently, taking a final deep breath
before they wake. It knows they will
fight and shifting; prepares
to shrink, compact the yelling—
until they stomp upstairs.
The house holds its breath
and cracks its joints,
nervous habits. I sit immersed in smoke,
Shooting Star incense—
a vigil for the valiant
efforts of the house. It contains
the anger within its bricks,
the secrets underneath the eaves.

"8:56 A.M. thoughts"
Silence permeates my mornings.
If I dare, I can let music notes linger in open air
and coffee complacently brew.
But instead I jab earbuds
into my ear and let
the only noise of my existence
be my footsteps on creaky wooden floor.
Some like to make an impact,
I tiptoe to hide my presence
so there's no mess behind me—
So when I leave, there is no sign
I ever touched ground.

"am i going to drown"
Sometimes I feel as if I'm
underwater. I look up
and feel as if I'm at the bottom of the sea–
everything looks leagues above me.
I settle into waves lapping against my skull
and accept I have reached the ocean floor;
I am going to drown.
I look around, see the sirens, and smile.
We sit in peace, until one of them
makes eye contact, and reaches out
their hand.

"surprised"
When your lips pressed against mine,
my heart yielded to yours.
I knew this was coming;
yet I couldn't anticipate the feeling
of your teeth biting my lip
Forgive me for gasping, but
the sensation caught me by surprise.
I have drifted on a monotonous existence
so long; you leave me breathless.

"tranquility"
Hello, is anyone there?
The music in my ears keeps my mind empty,
relief. Sweet silence, no worries occupy
my thoughts; heady tunes reverb
around my skull.
The calming numb spreads
through my fingertips, kissing
the nerves. Finally, I feel okay.
Such a pleasant change.
I slide my lids shut and let a smile
curve my lips as I welcome
what has been missing
for quite some time- tranquility.

"when are you coming home"
We wait like stones
in a river, waiting for the washout—
the relief of seeing your face
when you stumble through the door.
We sit in sagging couches,
wistful daisies rooted among napping kittens,
petals wilting as the hours tick by, growing stale
with your absence. Your cold shoulder presents pain
In a whole new light; when you hide away.
I was the one running away once.
Yet when the tables are turned; I can't make peace
with this limbo, the endless tapping my feet
as the minutes tick by. When are you coming
home?

"possibilities"
How wrong was it for my heart to suddenly
thud with adrenaline- excitement-
when I learned you had no strings attached?
Your puppetmaster has relinquished
all control. for the first time, I can have you
without the looming shape of her
gripping the nape of your neck.
We were electric once- wild and bright;
is it heartless of me to wonder
if we can make beautiful things
like we once did? Normally I would
seek the counsel of time, but dear,
we don't have much time left.
How tempting to let our passions root
and bloom as they may,
and maybe together we can grow
a neon garden again.

"a reason to say fuck love"
I am your fantasy. You see my long
Red hair and nose ring and curves
and murmur, "I would fuck her."
You imagine me under you, above you,
striking your senses and setting them ablaze.
I like to play with words sometimes; I consider
myself a someday poet. I have noticed
over the last couple days
that none of the letters in fuck are
In the word love. And maybe there
is a reason for that.
I am your fantasy. But you, you were
my future. And now that that has
been wasted, I think
I can never love again. Fuck.

"why I don't stand up straight anymore"
Powerless. I was unable
to stop it, the rude intrusion
into my dreams. I awoke to hands roaming
everywhere they shouldn't be
as everyone else slept untroubled.
How could I make waves
when I felt suffocated; how could I
ruin their sleep? After eternity
passed he stopped, but
not before he took the color
from my cheeks. I am nothing
but a wilted rose now.
I couldn't protect myself. My hands
were roughly held- my stem was broken.
And I was Powerless.

"when I realized leopards don't change their spots"
Here I go again-
bad habits chipping away
at my patchy psyche, trying to uncover
the rot my responsible behavior
has painted over. My morals
swoop and prepare to dive, lest I
draw them from the brink. The question
is, will I save them
or
let them slip carelessly
through reluctant fingers?

"can i pick myself up"
Here i sit- loneliness banging
against my temples. The city calls;
I tilt my head to listen.
Pressure on my skull builds,
intensifies. The siren song
of busyness beckons, lingers on stale air.
But sitting among quicksand sorrows,
I do not know if I can join the dance.

"a jarring sensation"
Why did you grab me,
a solitary koi fish, content to
swim in my lonely pond, and kiss
life into my burning gills?
I thrived beneath the surface
treading water, hiding amidst
the rocks of my whims and fancies.
Your world felt far above me, I knew
you shouldn't dip your hand into my water.
Yet there I lay–
gasping for air in your hands, and
you resuscitated me.

"what happens over time"
We were puzzle pieces, mismatched colors
yet somehow a perfect fit.
My light interlocked snugly with
your shadow, I sang the high notes
to supplement your low,
until you cried out of tune
and I no longer knew the words.
Our melody fell to shit.
That's what happens when
darkness swallows the sun–
tt was the end of times and
we had warped out of shape.
Desperately jamming ourselves
towards each other, we realized
we no longer fit.

"The aftermath"
You might not have foreseen this,
but when I find you,
you might notice your rope
knotted around my neck.
It's not a perfect size;
somedays the loop chokes me.
Other times, I slip my fingers
through the millimeters of space
between the twine and my neck,
and I can smell your cologne.
Dare me to tug the end, I beg you.
You might not have foreseen this,
but one plus one equals two.
Your actions forever lassoed me to you.

"Hidden treasure"
Can I duck behind your eyelids and
read the volumes of unspoken dreams contained
in your neurons again?
You think they don't amount to much,
as if you are on clearance, sold as is.
I long to confront the ones who have
convinced you your worth has diminished over the years,
as if you are a torn old couch, stained and holey
from the hard use of people who didn't recognize
your comfort and warmth until
it was no longer offered. I have sat in this one spot
with you, even if you are light years away,
and I have worn a nest for my body to curl into.
Your chest and hips form a shelter that your arms complete,
shielding me from the storms of the world as we sleep.
I will not leave you for the garbage men to collect.
With my two hands, I will sew together the holes,
recover you with a bright color
and plump your pillows. You are my centerpiece,
the missing piece in my living set.

Biography:

Morgan Rosati is a 23 year old from St. Louis, Missouri. After publishing a novela called *Shots, Lies, and that Party* in 2013, she took a step back from the publishing world. She didn't, however, stop writing. Amassing a giant selection of poems frantically penned on whatever paper available at the time or furtively typed in her Notes app, Rosati decided to put together a collection of poems. She hopes that people will relate to and empathize with the tumultuous time in her personal life during which she wrote most of the poems. Other than writing, Rosati likes to paint, read, and scrapbook. She has two wonderful daughters and a goofy nerd husband.